Caught by Rabroar

Written and Illustrated by Gwen Petreman

Edited by Erich Jacoby-Hawkins

Printed in the United States of America.

ISBN: 978-1-4669-5098-6(sc)

ISBN: 978-1-4669-5097-9(e)

Trafford rev. 11/14/2012

Trafford
PUBLISHING® www.trafford.com

North America & international
toll-free: 1 888 232 4444 (USA & Canada)
phone: 250 383 6864 ♦ fax: 812 355 4082

Tibbar loved to cook. There was nothing that made Tibbar happier than hopping through the valley searching for plants for his meals. When Tibbar ventured out on his own he had to be extremely careful. He constantly had to perk up his tall ears to listen intently for footsteps – special footsteps that belonged to none other than Rabroar.

Rabroar was huge and hairy. His whole body was covered with curly, red hair. Rabroar's favorite food was rabbits! He was so huge that he needed several rabbits a week to keep his stomach full.

Years ago thousands of rabbits had lived in the valley, but now there were fewer than fifty rabbits left.

It was Rabroar's nails which sent terror into the hearts of all the rabbits. His nails were long, pointed, and very sharp.

After the third rabbit had been devoured by Rabroar in a single week, all the rabbits were terrified to venture out of their warrens to look for food. None of them could escape the valley as it was surrounded by high mountains.

Then Tibbar came up with an idea. He suggested to the leader of the warrens that the rabbits should grow their own vegetables close to their burrows.

All the rabbits agreed that creating a community garden was a great idea! They all took turns standing on guard, while some dug the garden, planted the seeds, and weeded the vegetables.

One evening, just as Tibbar was ready to leave the garden, dark menacing clouds raced across the sky. In no time the garden disappeared behind sheets of pelting raindrops. As Tibbar felt his way through the blinding rain, he suddenly found himself gasping for air! Someone was lifting him high off the ground. Like a thunderbolt it struck him. Rabroar had caught him with his terrifying claws!

In no time at all Rabroar had carried him to his den.

Rabroar stared at Tibbar and roared, "**I AM STARVING! I'M GOING TO EAT YOU RIGHT NOW!**"

"Wait! Hold on!" cried Tibbar. "Please let me go back and say goodbye to my mom and dad and all my friends!"

Rabroar convulsed with laughter, "**Ha! Ha! Ha!** I see what you are planning. You are going to let me eat **your friends**, aren't you? I bet you figured that after I eat all your friends, I'll be too full to eat you! Ha! Ha! Ha! That's a great plan. I'll come with you. **I'm starving**!" declared Rabroar.

And away they went to Tibbar's warren.

"You'll have to promise to hide in another room while I make a delicious rabbit stew-just for you!" ordered Tibbar.

"Well, I've never had rabbit stew before. Okay! I promise! I'll spare your life. And I'll eat only your friends. Go ahead and turn them into rabbit stew," replied Rabroar.

As soon as Rabroar left to hide in another room, Tibbar began to make what he hoped would be the most delicious stew he had ever prepared in his whole life.

He worked frantically for about 40 minutes. After everything had been completed, he ladled the stew into an enormous bowl and placed a large carrot cake on a huge platter. In a quivering voice, he asked Rabroar to enter.

"Your rabbit stew is ready. You'll love it!"

Rabroar scooped an enormous pile of food into his mouth. He chewed it really quickly. Then he took another huge mouthful, then another, and another. It took him about five minutes to gobble down everything in his bowl. He then stared at the huge platter with the enormous carrot cake.

"What's that?" Rabroar asked pointing to the carrot cake.

"That's a – a rabbit cake!" answered Tibbar in a trembling voice as he slowly pushed the platter towards Rabroar.

Tibbar's heart was pounding so loudly, he thought for sure that Rabroar could hear every beat. His mind was racing! Please, please let him like all the food! If he hates it, I'm in big trouble! All the rabbits in the warren will blame me for bringing Rabroar to their homes. They will hate me! No one will ever speak to me again! Consumed with fear, he watched Rabroar grab a piece of cake.

S-l-o-w-l-y Rabroar began to eat the carrot cake. While loudly smacking his lips, he opened his mouth wide as he shoved one huge piece of carrot cake after another into his mouth. When he was finally done, Rabroar stood up with such force his stool went flying across the floor. Tibbar froze with terror when Rabroar once again grabbed him around his neck. As he was gasping for air, Tibbar could not believe what he heard!

"I love rabbit stew! I love rabbit cake! That was the most delicious food I have ever tasted!"

Rabroar suddenly stopped talking. He scratched his head. Then he got a very sneaky look on his face.

"You'll come to my cave! You'll live with me!"

"But – but why?" asked Tibbar in a trembling voice.

"You'll be my cook! I'll catch the rabbits! You'll turn the rabbits into rabbit stew and rabbit cake. You'll spend the rest of your life with me!" declared Rabroar.

Tibbar yelled, "Hold on! Just wait a minute! I- I have a confession to – to make."

"What are you talking about?" cried Rabroar.

"You – you did <u>not</u> eat rabbit stew! And you did <u>not</u> eat rabbit cake!"

Tibbar explained to Rabroar that he had used nothing but the veggies grown in the community garden. He told Rabroar how he would have enough food for the rest of his life, if he stopped eating rabbits and started to eat vegetables.

"I don't believe you! There is no way that veggies can taste so – so delicious!" declared Rabroar in a loud voice.

"I'm telling you the truth! Come and see for yourself. I'll show you our community garden and you can meet all my friends. I would never, never have let you eat my friends! If you join us, you can grow your favorite veggies. And you'll never go hungry again!" declared Tibbar.

When they arrived at the community garden Rabroar stared in wonder at two small rabbits pulling huge, purple carrots from the dark soil.

Tibbar couldn't believe his ears when he heard Rabroar's reply.

"I don't want to die of starvation when I've eaten all the rabbits. I'll do what you ask of me. With my long and sharp nails, I'll be the best digger and weeder you'll ever have!" bellowed Rabroar.

With Rabroar's help they harvested all the vegetables well before the snow fell. They celebrated with a huge feast. Tibbar made Rabroar his favorite dessert – carrot cake. After eating a whole carrot cake, Rabroar still wanted more. So the younger rabbits readily gave him their carrot cake in return for a bouncy piggyback ride on Rabroar's huge shoulders.

When the party came to an end, Rabroar lumbered over to Tibbar. He looked very stern and serious. For a minute Tibbar was almost afraid of him again.

Rabroar cleared his throat, "I was wondering if it wouldn't be too much trouble, could you please teach me how to make carrot cake?" asked Rabroar.

Tibbar giggled with relief.

"I'll teach you how to cook anything you want, if it means you'll never eat another rabbit as long as you live," replied Tibbar.

"I promise I will never eat another rabbit as long as I live," laughed Rabroar.

THE END

Fascinating Facts About Rabbits

There are 28 different species of rabbits.

Tibbar is an Eastern Cottontail which is the most common rabbit in North America.

Rabbits will live in many different areas such as the edge of woody areas, brushy hedgerows, and they will even live in suburbs and urban areas!

Wild rabbits have a great sense of smell and have excellent eyesight.

All rabbits can swim and the swamp rabbit will actually hide underwater from its predators!

They do not sweat but radiate heat from their large ears.

Rabbits are great jumpers.

They can jump about 1 meter high (36 inches).

Food

All wild rabbits are herbivores.

Since they are nocturnal they come out at night to look for grasses, twigs, shrubs, leaves, and other plants.

To keep rabbits from eating their veggies, some people plant a border of marigolds around their garden. Rabbits do **not** eat marigolds.

Wild rabbits rarely have to drink water from a pond or creek.

They get most of their liquid from dew and the plants they eat.

When rabbits poop they produce two kinds of droppings.

One kind of droppings is soft and the other is hard.

They need to eat their partially digested droppings to get enough nutrients.

Rabbits do not eat the hard droppings.

You can find rabbits searching for buds, twigs, and bark in winter, as they do not hibernate.

Family Names

Did you know that a mother rabbit is called a doe?

Can you guess what the father rabbit is called?

If you said buck, you are correct.

You probably predicted that a baby rabbit is called a fawn – but you are wrong.

A baby rabbit is called a kit or a kitten.

Maybe the reason that baby rabbits are called kittens is because they can purr like cats. If rabbits are frightened they will squeal.

A group of rabbits is called a herd.

Families

In the wild, a single rabbit lives in a den called a burrow. Family groups of 8 to 15 rabbits live in a series of burrows called a warren.

The female rabbits pull fur from their bodies to help make their nests so they are soft and cozy for the newborn kittens.

Rabbits are known for having lots of babies.

They will have babies as early as February and right up to September.

Baby rabbits are born hairless and with their eyes closed.

In about 6-10 days they will open their eyes.

They drink milk from their mother for the first 2 months.

The mother rabbit's milk is so rich she only has to feed her babies once or twice a day.

When a doe gives birth to a number of babies we call the babies a litter.

A wild rabbit's litter ranges from 2 to 10.

There has been a record of one rabbit having 24 kits!

Life Expectancy

Cottontails usually live for about two years in the wild.

A pet rabbit can live up to 10 years.

Wild rabbits can usually outrun most predators.

Many rabbits die when their ground nests get flooded.

A rabbit's teeth never stop growing.

Who do you think has more teeth – humans or rabbits?

Humans have 32 teeth while rabbits have 28 teeth.

Rabbits love to chew!

Enemies

Wild rabbits have many enemies.

Wild rabbits are prey to badgers, coyotes, eagles, foxes, hawks, owls, snakes, and wolves.

Some people will hunt and kill rabbits for their meat and fur.

Wild rabbits can try to escape from a predator by looking behind them and by running in a zigzag pattern.

They can run as fast as 20 miles (32 km) an hour!

They can also get away from predators by burrowing underground to hide.

If a rabbit gets caught out in the open it will sit extremely still hoping to avoid being detected.

Sometimes a rabbit has been seen to fight a predator by kicking it with its hind legs.

Staying Healthy Like Tibbar

Tibbar is a herbivore. That means he eats nothing but plants. Rabroar was a carnivore. That means he ate nothing but meat. Tibbar managed to turn Rabroar into a herbivore.

Most people are omnivores. That means they eat plant-based food and meat from animals.

A lot of people who want to stay as strong and healthy as possible, eat lots of fruits, vegetables, nuts, seeds, legumes, yogurt, and just a little bit of meat.

Some people never eat beef. They say that cows use too much good land, they drink too much of our precious water, and when they burp and pass gas they create a nasty greenhouse gas called methane.

People who want to stay healthy and energetic check labels on food very carefully. They do not want to eat processed foods or drink soft drinks that are loaded with either too much sugar or too much salt. They will make an earnest effort to avoid foods that have artificial coloring, artificial flavoring, artificial sweeteners, corn syrup, MSG (monosodium glutamate), olestra and trans fats.

The artificial color called carmine is actually made from bugs! The shiny coating on some candies, believe it or not, comes from the secretions of a bug called the lac beetle. This substance is also known as shellac and is used to varnish wood.

Tibbar's Easy- Breezy Nutritious Veggie Stew

1 large onion, chopped	5 garlic cloves, minced
5 or more of your favorite veggies cut into small pieces	1 tablespoon coconut oil
1 large can of diced tomatoes	1 large can cooked lentils
3 cups vegetable broth	1 teaspoon dried oregano
1 teaspoon dried basil	1 teaspoon fennel seeds
1 teaspoon freshly ground pepper	1 teaspoon rosemary
1 bunch fresh parsley	½ teaspoon sea salt

Instructions

1. Cook the onions with coconut oil in a large pan until they begin to brown.
2. Add the garlic and stir for another minute.
3. Add the rest of the ingredients except parsley and cook until the vegetables broth begins to boil. Add more salt or pepper if needed.
4. Cook 30 minutes on low.
5. Serve hot, garnished with parsley.

Tibbar's No Sugar Carrot Cake

6 cups grated carrots	½ teaspoon salt
1 cup dried cranberries	1 cup flaked coconut
4 eggs	4 cups grated apples
1 cup chopped walnuts	1 cup maple syrup
2 cups all-purpose flour	1 cup crushed pineapple, drained
1 cup coconut oil	2 teaspoons vanilla extract
1 ½ teaspoon baking soda	2 teaspoons ground cinnamon

Maple Syrup Sauce

1 cup Greek yogurt

1/3 cup frozen orange juice

1/3 cup pure maple syrup

Mix the ingredients together until smooth.

Instructions

1. Preheat oven to 350 degrees F (175 degrees C).
2. In a bowl, combine grated carrots , grated apples , and maple syrup.
3. Set aside for 1 hour, then stir in dried cranberries.
4. Grease and flour two 10-inch cake pans.
5. In a large bowl, beat eggs until light.
6. Gradually beat in coconut oil and vanilla. Stir in the pineapple.
7. Combine the flour, baking soda, flaked coconut, salt, and cinnamon. Add to pineapple mixture.
8. Finally, stir in the grated carrots, grated apples, maple syrup, and walnuts.
9. Pour evenly into prepared pans.
10. Bake for 45 to 50 minutes in a preheated oven until cake tests done with a toothpick.
11. Cool for 10 minutes before removing from pan.
12. When completely cooled, drench with maple syrup sauce.

CPSIA information can be obtained
at www.ICGtesting.com
Printed in the USA
LVIC052151180113

316381LV00004BA

9 781466 950986